This book belongs to

_____

DISNEY · PIXAR

A READ-ALOUD STORYBOOK

ILLUSTRATED BY
STUDIO IBOIX AND
THE DISNEY STORYBOOK ARTISTS

Random House 🏠 New York

Copyright © 2009 Disney Enterprises, Inc./Pixar. Original *Toy Story* elements © Disney Enterprises, Inc.
Slinky® Dog is a registered trademark of Poof-Slinky, Inc. © Poof-Slinky, Inc. Tinkertoy® is a registered
trademark of Hasbro, Inc. Used with permission. © Hasbro, Inc. All rights reserved. Mr. Potato Head® is a
registered trademark of Hasbro, Inc. Used with permission. © Hasbro, Inc. All rights reserved. Playskool Nursery
Monitor® is a registered trademark of Hasbro, Inc. Used with permission. © Hasbro, Inc. All rights reserved.
Playskool Rockin' Robot® is a registered trademark of Hasbro, Inc. Used with permission. © Hasbro, Inc. All rights
reserved. Fire Truck® by Little Tikes® and Toddle Tots® by Little Tikes® © The Little Tikes Company. Pez® is a
registered trademark of Pez Candy, Inc. Used with permission. All rights reserved. Etch A Sketch
© The Ohio Art Company. Published in the United States by Random House Children's Books, a division of
Random House, Inc., 1745 Broadway, New York, NY 10019, and in Canada by Random House of Canada Limited,
Toronto, in conjunction with Disney Enterprises, Inc. Random House and the colophon are
registered trademarks of Random House, Inc.
Library of Congress Control Number: 2008934586   ISBN: 978-0-7364-2595-7

www.randomhouse.com/kids

Printed in the United States of America

10 9 8 7 6 5 4

Andy was a young boy with many toys. He loved playing with them all, but his favorite was Sheriff Woody, a pull-string cowboy. Woody even had his own special spot on Andy's bed.

One day, Andy's mom called up to his bedroom. "Andy! Your friends are going to be here any minute."

"It's party time! See you later, Woody," Andy said as he dropped Woody off and headed downstairs with his little sister, Molly.

The room was quiet for a moment. Then Woody sat up and rubbed his head.

"Okay, everybody, coast is clear!" he shouted.

One by one, Andy's toys began to peek out of the closet, from under the bed, and out of the toy chest. They looked around, stretched, and began talking—something they could only do when there were no humans around to see them.

Woody gathered the toys together. He had important news.

First, Woody reminded the toys that Andy and his family would be moving to a new house in just one week. Then Woody blurted out the big news: "Andy's birthday party has been moved to today."

All the toys started squeaking and shouting at once! Birthday parties meant new toys for Andy, and everyone was afraid they might be replaced.

Woody sent the Green Army Men downstairs to spy on Andy's party. "Sergeant, establish a recon post downstairs. Code Red!"

Using a baby monitor, the soldiers were able to broadcast a description of each present to Woody and the other toys.

Luckily, nothing sounded too threatening . . . until the last present. All the kids gasped as Andy opened—

Just then, the baby monitor cut out. The toys were frantic to find out what the last present was!

Suddenly, Andy and his friends burst into the bedroom. Andy placed the mysterious new toy on his bed—right in Woody's special spot. Then all the children ran back downstairs.

Woody climbed back up onto the bed and introduced himself. "Howdy."

"I am Buzz Lightyear, Space Ranger," the new toy declared. Buzz said he was a space hero who had just landed on Earth. He also claimed that he could fly, and tried to prove it by bouncing off a ball. "To infinity . . . and beyond!" he shouted.

The other toys were impressed with Buzz's "flying." Woody merely rolled his eyes. "That's just falling with style," he complained.

After Buzz arrived, nothing was the same in Andy's room. Cowboy posters were replaced with space posters. And Andy stopped wearing his cowboy hat and started wearing a space costume instead.

The other toys liked Buzz, too. Everyone wanted to spend time with him—everyone except Woody.

Buzz was Andy's new
favorite toy, and poor
Woody was left in the toy
chest, alone and forgotten.

One evening, Andy's mom suggested going to Pizza Planet for dinner.
Andy could take only one toy, and Woody wanted to make sure he was chosen.
  Woody tried to knock Buzz behind the desk, where Andy wouldn't find
him. But instead, Buzz fell out the window.
  "It was an accident!" Woody tried to explain to the other toys.
  But they didn't believe him. They thought Woody had done it on purpose.

Just then, Andy ran into the room. He searched everywhere for Buzz.
When he couldn't find the space ranger, he grabbed Woody. Andy ran
downstairs and hopped into the car with Molly and his mother.

As the car started to pull out of the driveway, a small figure emerged
from the bushes and leaped onto the car's bumper. It was Buzz!

When Andy's mom stopped at a gas station, Buzz jumped into the back. "Buzz! You're alive!" Woody exclaimed in relief.

But Buzz wasn't as pleased to see Woody. "Even though you tried to terminate me, revenge is not an idea we promote on my planet," Buzz said. Then his eyes narrowed. "But we're not on my planet, are we?"

Buzz leaped onto Woody, and the two began pummeling each other. As the toys wrestled angrily, they tumbled out of the car and onto the pavement.

Suddenly, Andy's mom drove off. Woody and Buzz were stranded!

DINOCO

Luckily, Woody spotted a Pizza Planet delivery truck. The truck could take him and Buzz to Andy!

Woody's plan worked, and he and Buzz soon arrived at Pizza Planet. Woody figured they could jump into Molly's stroller and be home in no time.

"Okay, Buzz, get ready and . . . Buzz?" Woody turned around to see Buzz striding toward the Rocket Ship Crane Game.

Thinking it was a real spaceship, Buzz climbed into the game. Woody
followed. Inside, little green alien toys greeted the newcomers.

Suddenly, the machine's claw dropped—and it landed right on Buzz!

Woody tried to hold on to Buzz, but it was no use. They were both
pulled into the air and dropped into the prize slot.

"All right! Double prizes!" shouted the winner. Woody was horrified to
discover that it was Sid, Andy's mean neighbor.

Sid took Buzz and Woody home to his dark and eerie bedroom, where he liked to pull his toys apart and put them back together in all sorts of strange ways. These toys were mutants—and Buzz and Woody were terrified!

As Buzz and Woody tried to escape, Sid's vicious dog, Scud, chased them into separate rooms.

In the TV room, Buzz heard a voice. "Calling Buzz Lightyear! This is Star Command!" Buzz was about to respond when the voice continued: "The world's greatest superhero, now the world's greatest toy!"

It was a TV commercial for Buzz Lightyear *toys*!

Buzz was devastated to find out that he wasn't a real space ranger.

Back in Sid's room, Woody was desperate to escape. But Buzz was upset. He didn't even care when Sid found him and strapped a rocket to his back. Sid was planning to launch Buzz the next morning!

All night, Woody pleaded with Buzz to escape and return to Andy— before his family moved the next day. "Over in that house is a kid who thinks you are the greatest. And it's not because you're a space ranger. It's because you're his toy," Woody said.

Finally, Buzz understood that being a toy *was* important. He and Woody needed to get back to Andy!

As the two toys prepared to escape, Sid woke up. "Time for liftoff!" he yelled, grabbing Buzz and running outside.

Woody asked the mutant toys for help. "We'll have to break a few rules," he told them, explaining his plan. "But if it works, it'll help everyone."

Outside, Sid was getting ready to light the big rocket on Buzz's back when he heard . . .

"Reach for the sky!" called a voice. It was Woody, lying nearby.

Sid picked Woody up and examined the cowboy doll. At that moment, the mutant toys crawled out of their hiding spots around the backyard. Sid was surrounded!

"From now on, you must take good care of your toys. Because if you don't, we'll find out, Sid," Woody warned the boy. "So play nice!"

"AAAHH!" Sid shrieked in terror and ran into the house screaming.

The toys cheered—their plan had worked! Buzz was saved! And best of all, Sid's toy-torturing days were over.

But Buzz and Woody couldn't stand around and cheer. If they didn't hurry, the moving van—and Andy—would leave without them.

Quickly, the two toys ran toward Andy's house. Buzz couldn't fit through the fence because the rocket was still attached to his back.

"Just go, I'll catch up," he told Woody.

But Woody couldn't leave his friend behind. Woody helped Buzz squeeze through—but they were too late. Andy's family had already driven off.

Woody and Buzz dashed after the moving van. Buzz was able to climb onto the rear of the truck. As he tried to help Woody up, Scud came running down the street and bit Woody's leg, almost dragging him off the van.

"Nooooo!" Buzz yelled. He jumped onto Scud's head to save Woody.

Woody climbed safely onto the van, but Buzz was left behind with Scud. Woody desperately rummaged through Andy's toy boxes until he found RC, Andy's remote-controlled car. Using the remote control, he sent RC back for Buzz.

Andy's toys didn't understand that Woody was trying to save Buzz. They threw him off the van.

Luckily, Buzz and RC picked Woody up just in time . . . but then RC's batteries ran out.

Buzz and Woody watched the moving van drive farther and farther away. But then they realized that Buzz still had the rocket on his back!

They lit the rocket, and *zoom!* They flew forward so fast that RC landed in the van, while Buzz and Woody shot up into the sky.

Buzz snapped open his space wings, separating the rocket from his back just as it was about to explode.

"Buzz, you're flying!" Woody exclaimed.

"This isn't flying," Buzz replied. "This is falling with style!"

Buzz and Woody glided down toward Andy's car. The two dropped through the car's sunroof and landed safely on the backseat.

"Woody! Buzz!" Andy shouted. He hugged them close, thrilled to have his two favorite toys back.

Woody and Buzz couldn't have been happier.

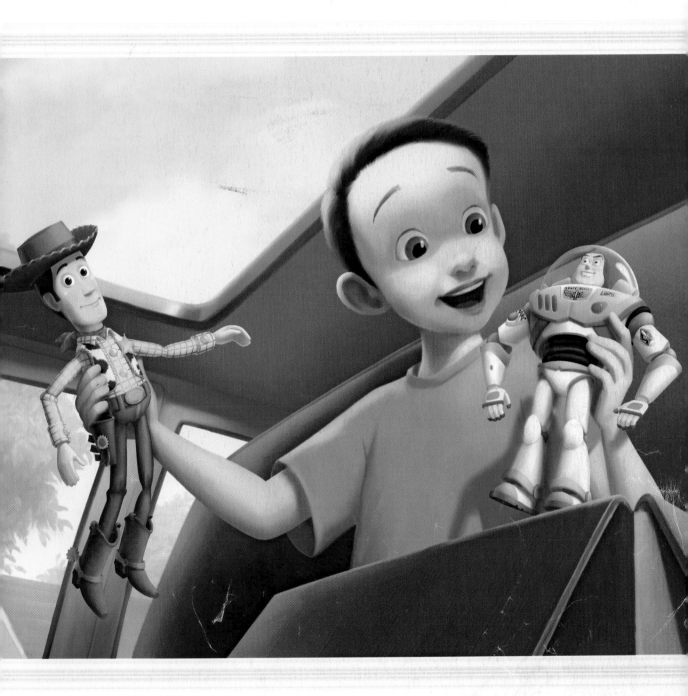

Andy, his family, and all his toys settled happily into the new house. Soon it was Christmas—and that meant new toys.

"You aren't worried, are you?" Woody asked Buzz.

"No, no," Buzz replied anxiously. "Are you?"

"Now, Buzz, what could Andy possibly get that is worse than you?" Woody teased.

Andy unwrapped his first present. Buzz's and Woody's eyes widened as they heard an unmistakable *WOOF-WOOF-WOOF!*

"Wow! A puppy!" Andy cried.

"**H**ey, Woody! Ready to go to Cowboy Camp?" Andy shouted, bursting into the bedroom.

With a few spare minutes before he had to leave, Andy grabbed Woody and Buzz for a quick adventure. "Never tangle with the unstoppable duo of Woody and Buzz Lightyear!" he cried, twisting the toys' arms together.

Suddenly, there was a loud *RIIIPPPP!*

Woody's shoulder had torn!

Andy's mom suggested fixing Woody on the way to camp, but Andy shook his head and sighed. "No, just leave him."

"I'm sorry," his mom replied. "But you know toys don't last forever."

Buzz and the rest of the toys watched in disbelief as Andy left without Woody. But Woody just sat sadly on the shelf with Wheezy, a toy penguin who had been left there alone for months, broken and forgotten. Was that Woody's future, too?

Suddenly, the toys spotted something truly terrifying—
Andy's mom was putting a sign outside: YARD SALE!

Unfortunately, she chose Wheezy as one of the sale items. Thinking
quickly, Woody waited till Andy's mom was out of sight. Then he whistled
for Buster, Andy's friendly puppy. Together they sneaked outside, grabbed
Wheezy, and headed back to safety. But because his arm was torn, Woody
lost his grip on Buster and tumbled to the ground.

Then a strange man noticed Woody, picked him up . . . and *stole* him!

Buzz jumped out the window and slid down the drainpipe, racing to rescue his friend. But he was too late.

All Buzz saw was the license plate LZTYBRN and a few feathers floating in the air as the car sped away with Woody.

Meanwhile, the strange man took Woody to a
high-rise apartment building. When the man left,
Woody tried to escape. But it was no use. He
was trapped.

POP! A box suddenly burst open, and Woody
was knocked off his feet by a galloping toy horse.

"Yee-haw! It's really you!" shouted a toy
cowgirl, squeezing Woody in a big hug.

The cowgirl said her name was Jessie and the
horse was Bullseye. Then she introduced the
Prospector, a toy who had never been out of his box.
They were all thrilled to see Woody.

"We've waited countless years for this day," said
the Prospector.

Back in Andy's room, Buzz and the other toys were trying to figure out who had taken Woody. The only clues they had were the license plate LZTYBRN and the feathers.

Buzz finally realized that the man had to be the goofy toy salesman on TV who owned Al's Toy Barn—and who dressed in a chicken suit!

Buzz decided to lead a rescue party to the toy store to save his friend. That evening, with a little help from Slinky, the toys jumped off the roof of Andy's house.

"To Al's Toy Barn . . . and beyond!" Buzz cried.

At Al's apartment, Jessie showed Woody an old television show, *Woody's Roundup*. Jessie, Bullseye, and the Prospector were all in it. And Woody was the star!

Jessie also led Woody through Al's room full of Roundup collectibles. Woody had fun exploring the collection with Jessie and Bullseye. They even danced on an old record player!

The Prospector explained that the Roundup toys had become valuable collector's items. Al planned to sell the Prospector, Jessie, Bullseye, and Woody to a museum in Japan. But the deal would only work if the toys went as a complete set.

By early morning, Buzz and his rescue team had almost reached Al's Toy Barn. All they had to do was cross one last, very busy street.

Luckily, Buzz noticed a pile of orange traffic cones. Slowly, the toys ventured across the street. Each one hid under a different cone.

Soon the street was filled with skidding, honking, crashing cars, all trying to avoid the strange moving traffic cones. But the toys barely noticed the pileup. They'd arrived at Al's Toy Barn.

Inside Al's Toy Barn, rows of shiny new toys seemed to stretch into the distance. Everyone looked up in awe—how would they ever find Woody here?

Turning a corner, Buzz discovered an aisle full of brand-new Buzz Lightyear toys. Suddenly, a hand clamped onto his wrist. It was a *new* Buzz Lightyear, who believed he'd caught a rogue space ranger! Quickly, the new toy trapped Buzz in a box and set it on the shelf.

Then New Buzz ran to join Andy's toys—and not one of them realized they'd left the real Buzz behind.

Buzz broke free just in time to see Al head out the front door—with Andy's toys hiding inside his bag! As he raced to catch up, Buzz didn't notice a dark figure rising up from a toy box. It was an evil Emperor Zurg toy! "Destroy Buzz Lightyear!" Zurg growled.

Back at Al's apartment, Woody told Jessie that he couldn't go to the toy museum because he had to get back to Andy. Jessie sadly explained to Woody that she had had an owner once, too—a little girl named Emily who had grown up and abandoned her.

"You never forget kids like Emily or Andy," said Jessie. "But they forget you."

Woody began to worry that Andy would forget about him one day, too.

Meanwhile, Andy's toys—and New Buzz—hitched a ride to Al's building in Al's bag. They sneaked through the vents and charged into the apartment, knocking down Jessie and Bullseye. Thinking that Woody was in danger, they grabbed him and ran.

Woody explained that Jessie and Bullseye were his friends. Then the real Buzz showed up, confusing everyone. When everything had been sorted out, Buzz tried to convince Woody to leave.

"Woody, you're in danger here," said Buzz.

But Woody wanted to stay. The Roundup gang needed him to make
a complete set for the museum. Besides, what if Andy didn't want
Woody anymore?

"You're a toy!" Buzz said. "Life's only worth living if you're being loved
by a kid."

Sadly, Buzz left Woody behind, leading Andy's toys toward home. But
Woody soon realized that Buzz was right—he belonged with Andy.

Woody ran to the vent and called to Buzz and his friends. Then he turned to the Roundup gang. "Come with me," he said. "Andy will play with all of us, I know it!"

Jessie and Bullseye were excited . . . but the Prospector blocked their path! After a lifetime in his box, he was determined to go to the museum. "And no hand-me-down cowboy doll is gonna mess it up for me now!" he shouted.

Suddenly, they heard footsteps—Al was coming! Andy's toys and New Buzz hid as Al packed Woody and the Roundup gang into a green case and dashed out the door. He was late for his flight to Japan.

"Quick—to the elevator!" Buzz shouted. He and the toys ran to the elevator shaft, hoping to catch up.

Unfortunately, Emperor Zurg had followed Buzz. Now he blocked the way!

Zurg attacked the toys with his blaster as New Buzz fought back. Rex turned away, terrified—and knocked Zurg off the elevator with his tail!

Buzz and the toys finally made it to the ground floor, but Al had already jumped into his car and driven off. How would they rescue Woody now?

Andy's toys hopped into an empty Pizza Planet delivery truck that was idling nearby. Buzz steered while Hamm shifted gears and Slinky pushed the gas pedal.

Soon they were swerving through traffic, hot on the trail of Al's car.

Driving wildly, Buzz and the gang followed Al right to the airport entrance. They sneaked into the airport inside a pet carrier, following Al and his green case.

"We just need to find that case," Buzz explained.

They entered a huge room full of conveyor belts. Hundreds of bags and suitcases and boxes headed off in all directions!

Buzz finally found Al's case, but when he opened it, the Prospector wouldn't let Woody go without a fight. Luckily, Woody managed to escape. Then he and Buzz sent the Prospector packing.

Bullseye broke free, too. But poor Jessie was still stuck inside Al's case when it was loaded onto the plane. Woody sneaked onto the plane, too, and soon he and Jessie were trapped! As the plane began to speed down the runway, Woody and Jessie crawled through a hatch. They began to climb down to the wheels, but then Woody slipped! Luckily, Jessie grabbed his hand just in time.

Dangling in the air, Woody tried a daring trick. First, he twirled his pull-string and lassoed a bolt on the wheel. Then he gripped Jessie's hand, and . . .

. . . together, they swung down toward the tarmac, where Buzz and Bullseye caught them! Everyone was safe.

Watching the plane take off into the sky, Woody, Jessie, Buzz, and Bullseye danced and cheered. "That was definitely Woody's finest hour!" cried Jessie.

When Andy arrived home from Cowboy Camp, he was surprised by what he found. "New toys!" he cried. "Thanks, Mom!" Jessie and Bullseye had joined all his favorites. Andy couldn't wait to play with everyone!

Someday Andy would grow up, and maybe he wouldn't always play with toys. But Woody and Buzz knew there was no place they'd rather be than with Andy. Besides, they'd always have each other—for infinity . . . and beyond!